JAKE JELLICOE AND THE
DREAD PIRATE REDBEARD

Nadin is the author of *Maisie Morris and
ful Arkwrights, *Maisie Morris and the Whopping
ies and *Solomon Smee Versus the Monkeys*. *Jake
Jellicoe and the Dread Pirate Redbeard* is her fourth
book and was inspired by her seafaring roots.
"Although I grew up in dull Essex, my family are
all Cornish. I inherited from them a love of the
sea Many of the locations in the story, such as
ock Spit and Stinking Porth, are based on
*tual Cornish villages, where my father and
uncles (who all appear as sailors on board the
Flounder) lived as children."

na's previous jobs have included working
guard, a radio newsreader, an adviser to
e Minister and a wardrobe assistant –
hich time she washed the underpants of
nous people. Joanna lives in Bath.

Books by the same author

Maisie Morris and the Awful Arkwrights

Maisie Morris and the Whopping Lies

Solomon Smee Versus the Monkeys

Jake Jellicoe and the Dread Pirate Redbeard

JOANNA NADIN
ILLUSTRATED BY DAVID ROBERTS

WALKER
BOOKS

This is a work of fiction. Names, characters, places and incidents are either the product of the author's imagination or, if real, used fictitiously.

First published 2006 by Walker Books Ltd
87 Vauxhall Walk, London SE11 5HJ

2 4 6 8 10 9 7 5 3 1

Text © 2006 Joanna Nadin
Illustrations © 2006 David Roberts

The right of Joanna Nadin and David Roberts to be identified as author and illustrator respectively of this work has been asserted by them in accordance with the Copyright, Designs and Patents Act 1988

This book has been typeset in Cochin

Printed and bound in Great Britain by Creative Print and Design (Wales), Ebbw Vale

British Library Cataloguing in Publication Data:
a catalogue record for this book
is available from the British Library

ISBN-13: 978-0-7445-5786-2

ISBN-10: 0-7445-5786-0

www.walkerbooks.co.uk

For my parents,
who love the sea

Thin

Some people are born thin and no matter how many chips or chocolate bars they eat they stay skinny.

Some people want to be thin and go on faddy diets like half a grapefruit for every meal or dog biscuits on Wednesdays.

Jake Jellicoe was neither of these. Jake Jellicoe was thin because he didn't get enough to eat.

Jake Jellicoe

Jake Jellicoe was so thin that if he turned
sideways he almost disappeared. He was so
thin he dared not walk over drains or cracks in
the path in case he slipped through. At school he
was called horrible names like "stick insect". And
old women in the streets frowned and shook their
heads when they saw such a sickly-looking child.

The rest of Jake's family was no healthier.
There was Mrs Jellicoe, whose fingers were raw
from gutting herrings at the Stinking Bloater
every day.

There was Mr Jellicoe, who washed the floors
at the fish market and whose every inch of skin
smelt of old kippers no matter how hard he
scrubbed.

There was Grandpa Jellicoe, who everyone thought was as mad as a mongoose. There were the twins Ned and Fred, who never stopped complaining about their empty bellies. And there was little Lily, who was three years old but looked barely more than a baby.

The Jellicoes lived in a tall thin house on a narrow back street in Pollock Spit. The house was so small that Grandpa Jellicoe slept on a threadbare sofa in the kitchen, Ned, Fred and Lily slept amongst the socks and pants in a chest of drawers, and Jake slept on a shelf in the pantry – which was less cramped than it might sound as all the shelves were empty.

For breakfast they ate thin grey gruel, which looked and tasted like the sort of glue mean men make from boiling down animal bones.

For lunch they ate one piece of stale bread each, with no butter.

And for tea they ate fishhead soup. Sometimes Mrs Jellicoe added a dishrag for extra flavour.

At night, as he lay in the damp empty pantry, Jake didn't dream of monsters or cowboys or fighting in the foreign legion. He dreamt of jam.

Gloopy sweet stuff, thick with red fruit and sugar. Jake had never tasted jam, but he knew it would be delicious.

You might think that things could not get any worse for young Jake. That he is probably the poorest boy you have ever heard of and that nothing could be nastier than fishhead and dishrag soup.

But you'd be wrong. Because something was about to happen. Something so big and so incredible that Jake's pitiful life would never be the same again.

Another mouth to feed

Mrs Jellicoe lifted the lid off an old battered saucepan. As she did so a fat tear rolled slowly down her cheek and plopped into the murky soup inside.

"Not that stuff again, Ma," complained Ned.

"I'm sick of it," agreed Fred. "Why can't we have roast beef or rabbit like normal families?"

Mrs Jellicoe dropped the ladle to the floor with a clatter, sat down on a chair and sobbed.

"It's OK, Ma," said Jake. "We love fishheads, really we do." And he gave Ned and Fred a sharp kick each under the table. The twins scowled but clamped their mouths shut.

"That's not why she's crying, Jake," said Mr Jellicoe as he put his hand on his wife's shoulder. "Something dreadful has happened."

"Oooh – are we adopted and our real father is a rich baron who is going to take us back to his enormous house and give us big feather beds with gold bedsteads and a servant to wash our bottoms?" asked Ned excitedly.

"Or have you stolen the King's diamond-encrusted egg cup and we're going to have to go on the run to South America?" demanded Fred.

"Ssshh, you two pests," said Grandpa. "Let your poor pa speak."

Mr Jellicoe took a deep breath. "The thing is," he said, "you're going to have another baby brother or sister."

"Is that true, Ma?" gasped Jake. "Really?"

Mrs Jellicoe wiped her nose and nodded sadly.

"But that's not dreadful," said Grandpa. "A new baby is joyous. We must celebrate."

"We can call it George," said Ned.

"Or Georgina," said Fred.

"No," said Mr Jellicoe. "We can't afford it. There's not enough food for the mouths I have to feed already. One more is one too many. And the house is bursting – there's nowhere for it to sleep."

"The coal scuttle is empty," said Jake. "Or I could sleep outside."

But Mr Jellicoe shook his head.

"What will you do?" asked Jake quietly.

"I'm sorry, son," said Mr Jellicoe. "When the baby is born we will have to sell it. Then there'll be enough money for all of us to eat."

Jake gasped.

"Sell it? Never!" shouted Grandpa. "You can't sell your own child."

"You know we will love it for ever," said Mr Jellicoe. "As much as we love every one of you. But our minds are made up."

"If only I still had my fortune," said Grandpa, shaking his head. "I was rich, you know. Richer than in your wildest dreams. My hands dripped with jewellery and my pockets bulged with coins. If I were still rich I would pay you myself with gold guineas."

Mr Jellicoe shook his head. "Don't, Dad," he said. "It's no use."

"When will the baby be born, Ma?" asked Jake.

Mrs Jellicoe smiled sadly at her son. "August," she said.

Jake did some maths in his head (which he was so good at he had once won a ceramic turtle in an arithmetic competition at school). "In six months?" he said.

Mrs Jellicoe looked at her tummy and nodded. "Six months."

The plan

Now, you may like the idea of selling your baby brother or sister. Every time they steal your toys or put sticky handprints on your favourite comic you might think it was worth a few pence to be rid of them. But not Jake. However much Ned and Fred or baby Lily annoyed him, he would never dream of selling one of them.

"Six months," he said to himself as he lay on the pantry shelf that night. "Six months to get enough money to pay for a baby. But how?"

He thought and thought.

"I could get a night job sweeping chimneys!" he said. "I'm slim enough to climb up inside and swoosh out soot." But then he remembered that everyone used their fires at night and like as not he would get his bottom singed. So he thought again.

"I could put a stocking on my head and rob the Royal Bank of Nomansland."

But he knew that stealing was wrong and, anyway, Pollock Spit was so small and he was so skinny that whatever he did, everyone would know that it was him.

Jake sat up. "Then I shall have to go away from here," he said. "Yes, that's it. I shall run away to seek my fortune, and when I'm rich I'll come back and Ma can have all the babies she likes and we'll live in a gigantic house with beds for everyone and we'll eat jam for breakfast and lunch and tea."

Jake hopped down from his shelf and looked around for things to take with him. From his box of treasures he took a compass. From his secret biscuit tin he took a mouldy cracker he had been saving for Lily. Lastly he added a pair of clean pants for good measure. He put everything in his trouser pockets, then he slipped on his shoes and socks and tiptoed across the kitchen to the back door. He was halfway there when a hand reached out and grabbed him sharply.

Jake yelped.

"Jake, boy. Is that you?" An oil lamp swung into his face so that he squinted. It was Grandpa.

"Y–yes, Grandpa," said Jake.

"Crikey, lad, you gave me a fright. I nearly whopped you one, thinking you were a burglar. What are you up to at this time of night? You should be fast asleep doing some growing."

"Promise you won't tell, Grandpa," whispered Jake.

"I'll decide on that when I've heard what you're hatching. Come on, out with it."

Jake knew there was no point lying to Grandpa. He had better tell the truth.

"I'm running away, Grandpa," he said, "to seek my fortune so I can buy back the baby."

"Oh, Jake," said Grandpa, shaking his head. "Such a thoughtful boy. But you can't run away. Your poor ma will go spare."

"But if I don't do something she'll have to sell the baby and that'll be even worse," protested Jake. "Don't you see? I have to go."

Grandpa pondered this for a minute. "You know what, Jake? I think you're right. I think it's about time someone around here did something to change our luck. And by golly, you're the boy to do it. If I wasn't so old and bent, and slightly deaf in one ear, I'd come with you. Where are you going?"

"I don't know yet."

"Well, it had better be far away from here. There's nothing in Pollock Spit but fish and old fools like me," said Grandpa, laughing. "The world's your oyster, boy – find a big town where the streets are paved with gold."

"Were you really once rich, Grandpa?" asked Jake.

Grandpa nodded solemnly at Jake. "I was, boy. I was."

"What happened?"

"I used to work at the main docks in Stinking Porth, bringing in the fish off the big trawlers. One day I heard a voice behind me. Nothing funny about that, you might say – after all, the docks are a busy place. But this was different. The voice belonged to a giant turbot that was

sitting in a box waiting to be wheeled down to the Mayor's own mansion for a state dinner."

Jake's eyes were wide in the flickering light. "What did it say?"

"Well, that's the funniest thing," said Grandpa. "I haven't a clue. It was speaking Hebrew and I don't speak Hebrew. But it spoke all the same. I was so excited that when the man came to collect the fish I slipped the turbot inside my overalls."

"Then what?" asked Jake eagerly.

"Then I set myself up as the owner of the world's only Hebrew-speaking fish. People came from miles around to hear it talk, and paid for the pleasure as well."

"So where's the money now?" asked Jake. "And where's the turbot?"

"Oh, a terrible thing happened," said Grandpa. "Back then, the sea was infested with pirates who pillaged and looted every town along the coast. One day, a dreadful man with wild red hair and a raven as black as coal on his shoulder came to Stinking Porth and stole all my money and killed the turbot with his cutlass just for fun."

"So it's all gone," said Jake sadly.

"All gone," said Grandpa. "Except for this." And he rummaged in his pyjama pocket and pulled out a single gold coin.

"I've been saving it for an emergency," he said, pressing it into Jake's palm. "I was going to give it to your ma – but I think you'll be needing it more."

Jake clasped the coin tightly. He had never seen anything so precious in his life. Now it was his. "I'll guard it with my life," he said.

"No, Jake," said Grandpa. "Use it to save your life. If you need to."

Jake nodded.

"Now go," Grandpa told him. "Your ma and pa will be up in a few hours – but they'll think you're asleep and I'll not let on. You've got a good few hours to get as far away as you can."

Jake threw his arms around the old man. "Thank you."

"Good luck," said Grandpa and pushed him gently away. "Go on, boy. Go."

Jake slipped the coin into his jacket pocket. Then he turned and walked across the dark kitchen, out of the back door and down the narrow street. And he didn't once look behind him for fear he would change his mind.

Stinking Porth

Pollock Spit in February was freezing and wet. Jake wished he had worn an extra jersey or a pair of long johns to keep out the bitter wind that blew in off the sea.

"The world is my oyster." He repeated Grandpa's words to make himself feel better. But Jake didn't like oysters. He had tried one once and it tasted like chewy fishy snot. What sort of world was that? He looked up at the clock on the chapel. It was nearly midnight. His ma and pa would be up in six hours getting ready for work, so he had better start walking. But where? Jake thought of all the wondrous places in the world he could go to, like the Hanging Gardens of Babylon or the Dead Sea. But none of them was very near. There was only one place within a few hours walk of Pollock Spit – Stinking Porth.

"Well, that's where I'll go," said Jake. After all, Grandpa had made his fortune there with the talking turbot, and if Grandpa could do it then so could he. So, gathering all his courage, he marched out of the little town of Pollock Spit and towards Stinking Porth and his fortune.

Jake walked for three long hours in the night. He walked past damp sheep huddling under trees and damp sheep sleeping standing up. He walked past the hangman's noose where highwaymen and pirates once swung for their crimes. He walked past woods and hedgerows and fields in the pitch dark of the night until finally lights twinkled in the distance and he saw houses and tall spires and, on the horizon, ships' masts bobbing. Then he saw what he had been looking for. At the side of the road was a large ominous sign that said: WELCOME TO STINKING PORTH.

"I'm here," thought Jake excitedly. "My fortune awaits."

And he hurried into town.

But the further he walked, the less bold he felt. All around him were dark alleys, and doorways filled with strange smells and sounds that made Jake start with fright. His ma had always said that Stinking Porth was a dangerous place, full of bad men and unsavoury women and thieves who'd rob their own grandma to make money.

Jake looked at the ground expectantly. The streets weren't paved with gold at all. They were just old dirty cobbles. As he stared down, a large whiskery rat ran over his feet. Jake yelped and ran into the nearest doorway, huddling on the floor to escape the cold, wet street and the creatures that ran in it. He pulled his coat tighter around himself. Maybe his ma was right. Maybe Stinking Porth really was a dangerous place and he had made a terrible mistake. But it was too late. He had to make his fortune here and he had six months to do it.

"Six months," he said aloud. "Six months."

And he kept saying it until he fell into a cold, dreamless asleep.

"Oy, what do you think you're doing, boy?"

Jake felt something hard poking him in the ribs. He opened an eye. A large and fearsome woman with a face like a battered rooster was standing above him, a broom in one hand and a bucket of slops in the other. For a minute he couldn't remember where he was or what he was doing there. But then, in a flood, it came back to him. He checked in his jacket pocket for the gold coin. It was still there.

"Get along with you, before I send you down the sewer with the rest of the gutter rubbish," said the woman, waving the horrible bucket at him.

"Sorry, madam," said Jake as he scrambled to his feet.

"Ooh, listen to you," said the woman. "Think you're posh, do you? Well, there's nothing clever about sleeping in an undertaker's doorway."

Jake looked up at the swirly writing above the shop. GRIMWOOD AND BOWDERY – FUNERAL PARLOUR. He shuddered and moved out of the angry woman's way and into the street. He looked around him. Shops everywhere were opening up. Trolleys laden with boxes of fish clattered past him over the cobbles, trays of bright fruit soared high above his head on the hands of greengrocers' boys, and whole pigs and sheep were swung over butchers' shoulders to be turned into cutlets and chops and bacon.

And there, right in front of him, stood the most fantastic shop he had ever seen. OUGH AND SONS – BAKERS TO THE KING was painted across the window in gold lettering and, through the glass,

Jake could see piles of sticky cakes and biscuits and fresh hot bread. His tummy rumbled, but he had no money, only the gold coin. For a moment he thought of spending it. He could buy more food than he'd eaten in his entire life. He could have crumpets and gingerbread and French fancies. He could eat until he was so full and round he would have to be rolled down the street.

But the coin was to save his life, not to be wasted on breakfast, so instead he reached into his pocket and pulled out Lily's stale cracker. It had weevils in it rather than currants and a liberal covering of mould instead of being sprinkled with sugar, but it was food. Jake took a bite. As he chewed slowly and stared longingly at the baker's, he noticed a board hanging near the door. On it were rows of small oblong cards offering horses for sale or looking for second-hand carts. Some of them, Jake noticed, advertised jobs. He looked keenly.

"Undertaker's apprentice," he read. "Five groats a day. Must supply own black suit. Apply to Mr Grimwood." Jake thought of the scary woman and shook his head.

"Royal Emergency Animal Corps – deadly electric-eel specialist required. Rubber gloves supplied. Apply Colonel Snell at Stinking Porth Barracks." Jake shook his head again. He wasn't too keen on wild animals – especially the deadly kind.

Then, on the bottom right-hand corner of the board, something caught his eye. Handwritten in neat, swirly lettering it said:

WANTED
Cabin boy
aboard the good ship Flounder.
Must be small and nimble.
Bed, board and a share of the profits.
Apply Capt. Dreadnought.

A ship! On a ship he could sail far away and seek his fortune. Jake remembered the tales he had read in schoolbooks. Of lands rich with fruit trees, where parrots swooped and squawked and the sea was as warm as soup. This was it! And even if he didn't find his fortune, he'd still have a share of the profits to buy back the baby.

"The *Flounder*," he said to himself, testing it out. But then he had an awful thought. What if another boy had seen it? He had better get there double quick if he wanted this job. So, cramming the last of the cracker in his mouth, Jake ran down the street – past the fishmongers and their crates of cod and pollock, past the flower girls selling violets and pansies, past a chimney sweep and his sooty boys with singed trousers, and further on down into Stinking Porth, towards the smell of the sea and the docks.

The Flounder

The docks were a new world to Jake. All sorts of strange people passed him by. Men with shiny buckles on their shoes and wearing enormous hats. Women in bright dresses and lipstick, singing as they jostled for space. The harbour itself was packed tight with boats. Tall ships and tugs, schooners and steamers, sloops, and crabbers with lobster pots stacked high on board.

Then Jake saw it. A giant wooden hull with three masts that reached up to the sky. A faded lady stretched across the prow, warding off the perils of the sea. On its side its name was etched in flaking gold. Jake pushed through the crowds to the harbour's edge. Then he walked up the gangplank and onto the *Flounder*.

On the deck, coiling rope and sharpening knives, was an assortment of wild-looking men. Tattoos tumbled down their chests, which were bare despite the winter weather. Their hair was tied in pigtails and gold hoops hung from their ears.

"Hello," Jake said nervously. "I'm looking for Captain Dreadnought. Do you know where I might find him, please?"

The men turned to stare at him. "'Ark at 'is lovely vowels, Bill," said one of them, laughing.

"Speaks proper job," said another.

"Oo might you be?" asked an especially scary man with A FAIR WIND inked across his arm.

"I'm Jake," said Jake. "Jake Jellicoe."

"Are ye now?" said the scary man. "And what might you be wantin' with the Captain?"

"I'm looking for a job."

"What as? Ship's mascot?"

The men laughed.

"A bilge rat?" the tattooed man added.

"Leave off him, Calico," said a tall brown-faced man with a red neckerchief and kind smile. "He's done you no harm." He turned to Jake. "Come on," he said, taking him by the arm, "I'll show you to the Captain's cabin." And he led Jake past the laughing crew to a small hatch in the deck itself. "Follow me."

So Jake climbed through the hatch, down the wooden ladder and into the very bowels of the *Flounder*.

Captain Dreadnought

"This is it," said the sailor. And he showed Jake through a door into a magnificent wood-panelled room before disappearing back along the galley.

Jake looked around him. The walls were covered in star charts and maps of lands Jake had never heard of – far-flung places like Caracas and Timbuktu. On the desk were funny instruments with strange symbols, which looked as if they measured something, but what exactly, Jake didn't know. There was an oil lantern made of green glass, which gave everything an eerie glow. In the centre, under a glass dome, was a stuffed black bird with a pointed beak and beady eyes that stared straight at Jake and made

him shiver down his back. But where was the Captain?

"Hello?" Jake said. "Is anyone here?"

"Indeed there is," came the reply.

Jake gasped and swung round. There, lounging on an armchair in the corner of the cabin, was a broad-shouldered man with black hair and a curled moustache. He was dressed in white tights, shiny black boots and a blue coat trimmed with velvet. Captain Dreadnought!

The Captain yawned extravagantly, showing a gold tooth, which glinted in the darkness. "What do you want, boy?" he asked.

Jake pulled himself together. "I'm here for the job," he said. "As cabin boy."

Captain Dreadnought stood up. He was a very tall man indeed. He looked Jake up and down as if he were a farmer at a pig market. "You look a bit thin and weedy to me," he scoffed. "Are you strong enough?"

"I'm very strong," said Jake. "I can crack a walnut with my bare hands." Which was a trick Grandpa had shown him one Christmas long ago when a kind neighbour had given his family their leftovers as a present.

Captain Dreadnought sniffed, unimpressed. "Very well," he said. "But are you fast?"

"Faster than a hare," said Jake, which may have been true, even though Jake had never seen a hare in Pollock Spit, let alone raced one.

"Hmm," said the Captain. "Can you sleep in clothes so wet and cold that you'll think you're a fish lost in the icy waters of the North Pole?"

Jake wasn't sure he liked the sound of that, but he nodded anyway.

"Can you stomach a sea so rough you'll think your belly is in your mouth and your bottom is two miles back towards port?"

Jake pulled a face. It sounded awful. But again he nodded – he needed the job.

The Captain stared at Jake.

Jake stared back.

"Very well," said the Captain, eventually. "You'll need to sign articles."

"What's articles?" said Jake.

"Ship's rules," said Captain Dreadnought and he opened a drawer and pulled out a sheet of thick paper. "Sign here," he said, slapping it on the desk in front of Jake. "Before you change your mind."

Jake looked. The paper was covered with the same neat swirly writing as the advert at Ough and Sons. "I'd just like to read it first, if I may," said Jake. Grandpa had always told him never to sign anything without checking the small print.

"Read it?" spluttered Captain Dreadnought. "No one's ever done that before. You mean you can actually read, boy?"

"Yes," said Jake.

Captain Dreadnought looked shifty for a second. Then he seemed to pull himself together and smiled. "Go on, then. I've nothing to hide." He puffed out his chest.

Jake looked at the piece of paper.

"Article One," he read. "Any man that shall neglect his business shall suffer such punishment as the Captain sees fit."

That seemed fair.

"Article Two. If any sailor shall strike another he shall receive Moses' Law – 39 lashes on the back."

Well, Jake wasn't likely to hit anyone, being so small.

"Article Three. If any man shall steal from the Captain or crew he shall be marooned with a flagon of water and a pistol."

Crikey, thought Jake.

"Article Four. If any man shall keep a secret from the Captain he shall be keelhauled or forced to walk the plank."

"What's keelhauled?" asked Jake.

Captain Dreadnought smiled. "Dragged underwater and scraped across the barnacles on the bottom of the boat until you are blistered and sore."

Jake gulped. He was beginning to realize why the Captain had hoped he wouldn't bother to check it.

"Article Five," he continued. "If any man shall lose his right arm he shall receive 600 pieces of eight. For his left arm, 500 pieces of eight." The list went on with 400 gold coins for a left leg, down to 100 for an eye or finger. For both legs and arms the compensation was 800 pieces of eight and a servant.

"Call it an insurance policy," said Captain Dreadnought.

Jake stared in horror. But then he saw Article Six. "Food entitlement," it read. "A sailor's daily ration will be:

- ⚓ one pound of bread or biscuit
- ⚓ one pound of beef or mutton
- ⚓ an ounce of peas
- ⚓ an ounce of tea
- ⚓ half an ounce of sugar."

"Really?" asked Jake.

"Of course," the Captain replied. "A crew can't run on empty bellies."

Jake's mouth watered. This was more than his family ate in a year. "I'll do it," he said.

Captain Dreadnought smiled and handed him an inkpen. Jake signed his name carefully at the bottom of the articles.

"Well, Jake Jellicoe," said Captain Dreadnought reading the signature. "Welcome to the *Flounder*." And he rolled up the paper, put it back in the drawer and slammed it shut.

Then the Captain rang a brass bell on the wall.

A lean, tallow-faced man stepped into the cabin.

"This is Saggers," said the Captain, still smiling like a crocodile. "First Mate. He's in charge when I'm not on deck. You'll do as he says at all times."

"Come along, boy," said Saggers, his face as still and grey as a dead fish and his voice as cold as the sea itself.

"Goodbye, Jake," said Captain Dreadnought. "For now."

Jake was just about to follow Saggers out of the cabin when he thought of something. He turned back to the Captain, who was seated at his desk looking at a book of maps. "When do we sail?" Jake asked.

"Sail?" said Captain Dreadnought, closing the book with a sharp smack. "Why, Master Jellicoe, we sail tonight."

The crew

J ake followed Saggers back along the deck. The wild men had gone. Saggers walked him through the web of rope and lines, past the ship's masts that reached into the clouds to a sort of wooden hut with no windows. "This is it, boy," he said, opening a tiny door. "Your home for the next six months."

Jake looked in. There was a set of steep wooden steps leading down into a gloomy room. Well it was surely better than the shelf in the pantry.

"Get a move on, boy," said Saggers. And he pushed Jake forward, laughing a thin mean laugh as he slammed the door behind him.

Jake climbed carefully down the steps and then looked around him. The room was long and narrow, its walls lined with bunks and hammocks two high. There were no tables or chairs, just rings on the floor to which were lashed several large chests. Balanced on one was a single candle, which was barely bright enough to light up a small area around it.

"Where's your baggage, son?" said a voice behind him. Jake turned to see a red neckerchief and a familiar weathered face. It was the same kindly man who had taken him to see Captain Dreadnought.

"I haven't got any, sir," said Jake. "Just what's in my pockets."

"Fair enough," said the man. "And less of the 'Sir'. My name's William Baxter. Bill, to you. I'm the ship's carpenter. Welcome aboard, Jake. This man here in the bunk above you is Pip Lloyd." Jake looked up and saw another man, this one with a round happy face and a lot of hair. "He's the sailmaker. And over here's Jack Rackham – commonly known as Calico Jack." Jake recognized the man with the tattoo.

"Then there's Tom Lundy – tillerman," continued the kindly man, "Samuel Avery – he's in charge of guns, in case we meet any pirates or bandits out there – and Charley Farley, Richard Llewellyn and Christie Hammond – all Able Seamen."

Jake nodded hello to each of the crew in turn, some tall and gangly, others short and wiry, but all with weathered faces and the look of brave adventurers.

"And you've met Saggers, of course," added Bill. The rest of the crew hissed and made cat-calls. "All right, boys," said Bill. "Settle down. Now listen, Jake. Saggers is in charge when the

Captain's not about. You want to watch your step – he can be mean and brutal. But it's not his fault. He has to be like that. A ship's a dangerous place – one slip and we could all be facing death."

Jake was just contemplating what that slip might be when the ship's bell rang three times, followed by Saggers's voice shouting, "All hands on deck!"

"Come on, boys," said Bill. "Time to find out where this good ship's bound."

Jake's belly lurched with a mixture of excitement and fear. He was about to be told where his fortune lay. And, with his heart leaping inside him, he followed Bill and the crew up the steps, through the tiny door and onto the deck of the *Flounder*.

Captain Dreadnought stood with his legs wide apart and his arms behind his back. On one side of him stood Saggers, his face deadpan, and on the other, with her hands on her ample hips, was a short woman with enormous skirts, a lazy eye and grey, greasy hair that sat on top of her head like a dead squirrel. Around her feet a fat, hairy

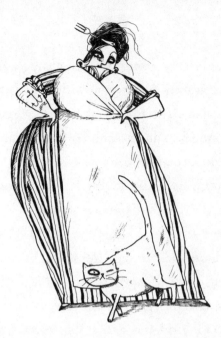

cat prowled. She had a look that suggested she might not be the most amiable of shipmates.

"Who's that?" he whispered to Bill.

"That's Mrs Grimes, the ship's cook."

Jake's tummy rumbled. "Is she like a chef?" he said, thinking she didn't look much like the jovial red-cheeked pie-maker he had imagined.

Bill laughed. "Not unless you like your beef hard-boiled and your eggs raw. She's the ship's doctor too. Mind you don't eat too much of her bad grub or you could find yourself getting a dose of her bad medicine as well."

Jake shivered, imagining her sausage-like fingers forcing milk of magnesia down his throat.

"Silence in the ranks!" shouted Saggers. Jake and Bill stood to attention. The first mate nodded at Captain Dreadnought, who smiled.

"My name is Captain Dick Dreadnought," he announced loudly and proudly. "Former Lieutenant in His Majesty's Navy. There is no ocean I haven't crossed, no sea I haven't sailed. I've been from Cape Horn to the Labrador Straits and back again, and never once have I sunk. You'll find me a fair captain, if you keep your watch and know your place. But if I'm crossed, you'll have Saggers here to deal with."

Saggers stared grimly at the crew.

"I expect by now you'll want to know where we're headed," the Captain continued.

There were nods and whispers among the crew.

Captain Dreadnought, who clearly knew what he was doing, paused to make his revelation seem all the more dramatic, then announced in a stage whisper, "We are going to find the lost treasure of the Dread Pirate Redbeard!"

There were gasps, then a brief hush before the questions started.

"But Captain," said Pip Lloyd. "Not wishin' to state the obvious, but it's lost."

"That's right," added Tom Lundy. "Ships have tried for years to find it and most have perished in the process."

"There's not even a map," piped up Charley Farley.

"We'll never do it," said Calico Jack. "We might as well go 'unting for the bearded snark."

"What's a bearded snark?" asked Christie Hammond.

"No idea," said Calico Jack. "I just made it up – that's what a waste of time it would be."

"Enough," said Captain Dreadnought, holding up a hand. "It is true that the original map was lost with Redbeard himself."

The hubbub rose again amongst the crew.

"Wait!" said the Captain. "I haven't finished yet. There was a second map – a copy – which is now in my possession."

The crew fell silent.

Captain Dreadnought smiled at the stunning

effect the speech was having on his audience. "But I must warn you, we are not the only ones looking for the loot. I have it on good authority that Redbeard's own mortal enemy, the fearsome Boris Kalashnikov, has been tipped off as to its whereabouts."

There were more gasps, but the Captain continued. "This will be a tough journey across treacherous waters and you may not all return. But if you do it'll be as rich men, because there's a share of the treasure for every one of you."

"Hurrah!" shouted the crew together.

"Hurrah!" added Jake, and his eyes lit up with delight. Treasure! There was treasure in it for him. Enough to buy the baby back for sure.

"But until then…" said Captain Dreadnought, swinging round to stare at Jake. "Until then, you belong to me, body and soul. Especially soul. Every last one of you."

Jake gulped.

Captain Dreadnought nodded at Saggers.

"Anchors aweigh!" shouted Saggers.

"Come on, Jake," said Bill. "This is where the work starts." And he grabbed hold of a sail rope.

Jake watched the others pick up their own coils and took one of his own.

"Yo heave ho!" shouted Pip Lloyd. And he began to sing a sea shanty.

The ship pulled out of port, the sailors heaving and singing in unison, the sails unfurling and rising up their masts, and Captain Dreadnought standing on the prow, gazing out to sea through his telescope. And as they sailed across the ocean, away from Stinking Porth and the dirty cobbled streets, away from Pollock Spit, with its damp foggy air and fishy smell, Jake dreamt of an island rich with rubies, where the gold lit up the night. This was it. There was no turning back now. He was off to seek his fortune.

All at sea

Jake was woken at dawn by the loud clanging of eight bells. He groaned, his arms aching terribly from all the heaving and hoing last night. He sat up in bed just as a pair of hairy feet appeared in front of his face.

"Yuck," said Jake to himself.

The feet jumped down to the cabin floor, with a bleary-eyed Pip Lloyd attached to them. He bent over and smiled at Jake. "Mornin', boy," he said. "Time fer breakfast. You'd better 'urry. Saggers don't like slugabeds."

Jake didn't want to get on the wrong side of Saggers so he hopped out of bed quickly. He had slept in his clothes – all the men did, in case of a storm in the night. All he had to do was pull on his shoes and he was ready. And golly, was he ready! All he had eaten in the last two days was Lily's mouldy cracker, and his tummy was growling and grumbling like a bear trapped in a sack.

But when he sat down at the long table in the galley he began to wonder whether he might be able to live on that cracker alone for the rest of the voyage. In front of him was a bowl of the same thin porridge he ate at home. But this one had strange lumps in it and something that looked remarkably like rat poo floating on the surface.

"What's wrong?" snapped Mrs Grimes, eyeing him suspiciously. "Not hungry? Food not good enough for you?"

"N–no, ma'am," stuttered Jake. "It's just… I think a rat might have done something in my bowl."

Mrs Grimes smiled nastily at him. "Them's just small raisins," she said. "Any more complaints from you and it'll be rat

you're eating, let alone its droppings." And she stamped back into the kitchen, her enormous skirts swishing as she went.

"Ignore her," muttered Bill, who was sat on Jake's left. "Her bark is worse than her bite. Here – give the porridge to the cat." He took the bowl and slid it under the table. "Ahab!" he called. The fat creature Jake had seen with Mrs Grimes yesterday came running across the floor, belly low to avoid inadvertent kicks from the other men.

"Will he eat it?" asked Jake.

"Why d'you think he's so fat?" asked Bill, laughing.

"'Ere, 'ave this instead," said Pip. And he slipped Jake something round and hard under the table.

Jake looked down. It was a bright red apple. "Where did you get it?" he asked in amazement.

"Captain's own store. But don't say a word. If anyone catches you, I'll say you nicked it," said Pip.

"I won't," said Jake and slipped the apple into his pocket for later.

"Pip's our own secret Quartermaster," laughed Bill. "Somehow he always manages to find a piece of fruit or a biscuit to eat."

"I wanted to be a cook meself," said Pip, wistfully. "But me dad said it was no job for a man, so I sews sails instead."

Jake nodded. "Tell me about Redbeard and the lost treasure," he said.

"Redbeard?" said Bill. "Blow me down. You mean to say you've never heard of the Dread Pirate Redbeard?"

Jake shook his head.

"Well, he was only the most ferocious pirate ever to sail the seven seas," said Bill. "He was more than six foot tall with wild red hair and ribbons in his beard. On his head he wore a hat that he stuffed with burning rope so he looked like the devil himself."

"They say he was raised by puffins after 'is own ma and pa abandoned him cos he was so bad," added Pip.

Bill nodded. "He sailed in a boat called the *Evil Edna* with a crew of thieves and robbers. Every one of them had done time in prison for hideous crimes."

"Crikey," said Jake.

"Any ship he came across, he'd kill the captain and crew and steal everything they had aboard. The decks of his ship had to be covered in sand to soak up all the blood and bits. And it was the same in the ports he sailed to. Pillaged and looted every one of them. If a lady refused to hand over her rings, he'd chop off her fingers and stick them on his hat, to warn others just how bad he was."

"What happened to his treasure?" asked Jake.

"Well, that's the thing," said Bill. "He was so greedy that all the booty he had amassed on board began to sink the ship. So to try and lighten her, he threw all the ship's supplies overboard. When that didn't work, he threw the crew over. But she was still sinking, So he decided to unload the treasure, then go back to port and get a bigger boat that could carry it all. He found a secret island, rowed ashore in his lifeboat and buried as much treasure as he could. He drew a map so he'd know where to find it, then hurried back to where he'd left his ship. But by the time he got there she was already sunk.

"Then what happened?" asked Jake excitedly. "Where's Redbeard now?"

"Well, that's the thing," sighed Bill. "No one really knows what happened. Some say his eyes were pecked out by gulls and he sailed blind across the seas in his lifeboat till he dried up into no more than bones. Some say he went back to the island where he'd buried the treasure and sat on the shore, waiting for a ship to come along. Day after day he waited but none ever came. All I know for sure is that he's in Davy Jones' Locker and that's the best place for him."

"What's Davy Jones' Locker?" asked Jake.

"It's where all dead sailors go," said Pip. "Forty fathoms down at the bottom of the sea, dark as night and cold as ice."

"How do you know all this?" asked Jake.

"I seen him once," said Bill, "when I was a cabin boy like you. It was him that took my dad away."

"Bill's dad was a ship's carpenter, like 'e is," said Pip.

Bill nodded. "This was long, long ago. Captain Redbeard had killed all his own crew, because he thought they was stealing off him. So he raided our ship and took my dad and some of the other men and forced them to sail the *Evil Edna*. Never saw my dad again." Bill shook his head. "Terrible man he were. I'll never forget that face … that red beard."

"I'm sorry," said Jake.

"Aye, well," sighed Bill.

"But at least the seas are safe now," said Jake, trying to cheer him up.

"Oh, that's where you're wrong, boy," said Bill, shaking his head. "Captain Redbeard had a mortal enemy – Boris Kalashnikov. And he is very much alive."

"Oh, 'e's terrible," said Pip. "Grates the soles of 'is victims' feet with a cheese grater and makes 'em eat the shavings."

"Then he lets rats nibble their ears and worms wriggle up their nostrils," said Tom, joining in.

"Then he scrapes his nails down a blackboard to really make 'em squirm and scream," added Charley.

"He's as wide as he is tall with a bushy beard the size of a small Alsatian," said Richard.

"You smell 'im before you see 'im, cos 'e never takes 'is shirt off to wash it, not till it's naught but threads," said Calico Jack.

"His crew have one eye apiece and hooks instead of hands," said Christie. "And they sail in a ship called the *Molotov*, which is painted entirely in black, even the insides, so any man who tries to plunder her gets lost and wanders in the darkness for days and days."

"Now, he's the most notorious of them all – the King of Pirates," said Bill. "He's who we have to watch out for now. You hear me, boy?"

"I do," said Jake, shuddering. "I do."

Sea legs

Over the next few days Jake learnt fast. He learnt words like longitude and circumnavigate, and that ships were always called "she". He learnt that port was left and starboard was right. He learnt to shout "watch under" when he was sick over the railings, which was often.

From Bill he learnt to sand and polish wood so it was watertight. Pip taught him to mend rips in sails and sing sea shanties, which always involved dead or drunken sailors and bottles of rum. Tom Lundy, the tillerman, taught him about the trade winds and the clouds that looked like mackerel, which all sailors were afraid of. Samuel Avery taught him how to keep gunpowder safe and dry. Calico Jack taught him to say insults in four different languages including Mandarin. And all the crew taught him to avoid Saggers.

Slowly the days stretched into weeks and the weeks into months, until Jake no longer threw up every time the sea heaved; until his face and arms and legs were as brown as Bill's; and until "fore upper topgallant halyard belayed to the pin third from aft on the starboard side" no longer sounded like gobbledegook.

When Jake wasn't busy learning, he liked to hear about the legends of the sea. All the crew had tales to tell of the enormous monsters and fearsome pirates they had encountered and beaten down. Jake never tired of them – though the tales became more elaborate with each telling. There were marvels like giant squid and whales so big they could devour an entire ship in a single bite. There were fabled lands, lost continents, cities sunk at sea and others made entirely of gold. There were magnetic islands that trapped ships by pulling at the iron nails in their wood and there were ghost ships that would sail right through you with only a strange shiver to let you know of their passage. Jake drank it all in as he would lemonade, but still he thirsted for more.

"Tell me again about the places you've been," he said one night, his legs dangling over the bunk as he watched Bill sharpening his penknife.

Bill looked up and grinned. "I've been places as hot as tar and others so cold your breath freezes before it's left your nostrils," he said. "I've seen things that would make you squirm with terror. I've seen an island where the hills were made of gold dust guarded by winged monkeys as large and vicious as ill-tempered hounds."

Jake was just about to ask why the monkeys didn't fly away from the island when the ship gave such an almighty lurch that he flew off his bunk and onto Bill's lap. At the same time, Pip tumbled off his bed and crashed onto the floor, knocking the candle out as he went, so that they were trapped in darkness.

"What was that?" said Bill.

"No idea," said Pip fearfully. The ship rolled again, sending everyone on top of him. "Ow," said Pip.

Then they heard a loud crack outside.

Thunder, thought Jake. He clambered to his feet, ran up the steps and flung open the hatch. Rain stung his face and lit the boat up in a flash of lightning. The deck was awash with water, ropes flapped and bells clanged and above him black clouds crashed into each other. "Storm!" he shouted to the men down below.

Bill and Pip and the others fought their way up the steps.

"Saggers'll kill us!" cried Bill. "We should have seen this coming. Look." He pointed at the barometer, which had dropped to "0".

"Whose watch was it?" asked Samuel.

Jake suddenly remembered. It was his. He had been so lost in Bill's tales that he had clean forgotten that he should have been on deck.

Bill caught his eye and shook his head. "Don't say a word," he whispered. Then he turned to the others. "Never mind that. Come on, there's work to be done. We've to save the *Flounder* or die along with her."

The storm

"There's nothing we can do now but ride the storm out!" shouted Bill above the noise.

"He's right," snapped a voice. It was Saggers. "But we need to reef in the sails first."

"Aye aye, sir," said Bill and nudged the others.

"Aye aye," they repeated.

"Slack off the sheets and pull 'em in!" shouted Saggers.

Bill, Pip and the rest of the men grabbed a sheetline each. Jake copied them.

"Heave!" cried the first mate, his voice rising above even the loudest shrieks of wind.

Waves crashed across the deck, threatening to wash them all out to sea. The clouds were now so

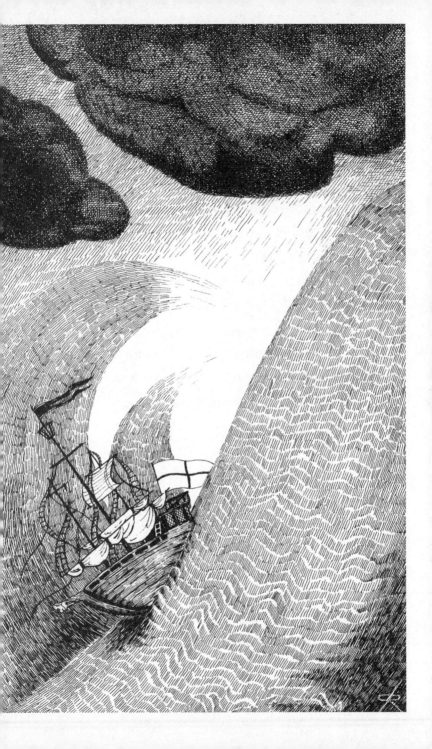

low that they engulfed the mastheads. Hail and rain was coming down thick and fast.

The *Flounder* pitched and rolled and still the men heaved. Jake's fingers were numb from the cold and his clothes were stuck to his skin with the rain, but still he pulled with the others. And they carried on pulling together until the sails were hauled in.

"That's it, men," said Saggers. "Now we'll have to furl 'em."

"What's that mean?" shouted Jake.

"It means some of us has to climb aloft and lash the sails to the yard before they blow themselves to rags or kills someone," said Bill.

"Who has to do that?" asked Jake.

"Bill," said Saggers, pointing at him. "You take the mizzen mast. Pip Lloyd, you take the jigger." Saggers looked around him, his eyes settling on Jake. "You, boy. You take the main mast."

"Come off it, Saggers," Bill protested. "He's never been up so high before, let alone climbed up in a storm."

"Shut up," snapped Saggers. "He'll do as I say. Now get going, boy. Unless you want this

66

ship to be your coffin."

Jake shook his head as the winds gusted across the deck. He looked up to the top of the foremast. However bad it was down here, Jake knew it would be worse up there.

"First thirty feet's the hardest," said Saggers. "After that a fall will kill you from any height – the only difference is the time you have to think about it on the way down."

Jake felt sick. Bill shot Saggers a look, then put his hand on Jake's shoulder. "Go on, boy," he said. "You can do it."

"Yeah – go on, Jake," nodded Pip. "We know you're as good a sailor as any of us."

Jake tried to smile but he was too scared.

"Get going," barked Saggers and pushed Jake against the mast.

Desperate to get away from the first mate, Jake grabbed hold of a rope and hauled himself up a little way. Then, slowly, hand over fist, his knees gripping tightly in between pulls, Jake climbed up the icy ratlines and footropes higher and higher into the raging storm. When he reached the yardarms he looked down. Bill and Pip were below him working at their own masts, hauling in the sails and tying them tight. Down on deck he could just make out the rest of the crew; they looked like specks of dust, insects he could crush beneath his foot. Above him he could see nothing but black cloud and rain. And all the time the wind buffeted him so that he swung side to side on his rope, his legs and shoulders jolting against the mast every few seconds.

Jake felt dizzy and scared. But if he didn't keep going then he knew the crew were goners. He reached out to grab one of the yardarms, but as he did so the wind caught him again and whipped him the other way. Jake screamed, but his voice was lost in the noise of the storm, just as his salty tears were washed away by the sea spray. He braced himself and tried again. This time he caught hold of the yardarm and swung his leg over. Then he let go of the rope and grasped the wood with both hands. "Nearly there," he said to himself. Below him, the sails, which looked light as bedsheets on a fair day, were now heavy with rain. Jake began to roll them in. He worked and worked at the heavy canvas, securing each sail before crawling back to the mast to move on to the next. The work took no more than a few minutes but to Jake it seemed like hours before he finally furled his last sail. He looked down to see Bill and Pip waving at him. Jake thought they might even have been cheering. But he couldn't hear above the noise of the sea. He hugged tight to the mast, breathing heavily with exhaustion and relief.

But he had to get down. Jake looked below again. Pip was back on deck, Bill was still in the rigging, waving. Jake waved back. Bill waved even more frantically. Suddenly Jake realized that he wasn't waving at all. He was pointing. Jake looked out to sea. Then he saw it. Higher than the clocktower on Pollock Spit Chapel, and higher than the top of the mast he was clinging to. It was a giant wave and it was heading straight for the *Flounder*.

The men hadn't been cheering, they had been

shouting! Jake scrambled down the rope as fast as he could, letting it slide through his fingers, no matter that it burnt the skin. By his reckoning the wave was only five seconds away. He knew the men would go down the hatch and lash it tight. Anyone above deck would be as good as dead.

Four seconds.

Jake was still a good way up.

Three seconds.

Bill had reached the deck by now, but Jake wouldn't make it. He knew it.

Two seconds.

It was no use. He was going to have to hold his breath and pray.

One second.

The hatch on the deck slammed shut. Jake closed his eyes and took a huge gulp of air. Then it hit. Jake felt the *Flounder* tip and fall. The mast was whizzing down and down towards the sea, which it hit with an almighty splash. But it didn't stop there – it kept on going. Jake clung to the mast as it sank beneath the waves. The sound of the storm disappeared and all he could hear was water whooshing in his ears as he plunged deeper into the ocean. Jake's lungs burned with the air held inside. He thought of all the stories of wrecks that the crew had told him. Of sailors trapped in holds as ships sank to the seabed. That was where Davy Jones' Locker was – down among the fishbones and the seaweed.

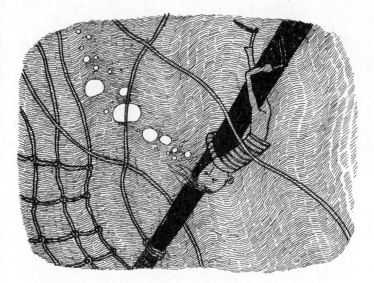

But just as he was contemplating certain death, Jake felt something strange happen. There was a sort of change in gravity. Instead of being pulled down, his body was whizzing back up again and then, as fast as he had been dragged under, he was flung up into the deafening sky, still clinging to the mast. Jake opened his eyes in disbelief. The *Flounder* had rolled right over. He was alive!

"We did it!" Jake yelled into the wind. "We did it!" He whooped and shouted for all he was worth.

Down on the deck below, the hatch swung open and Bill's face appeared, followed by Pip and Sam and the others.

"By crikey!" cried Bill. "Jake Jellicoe is alive!"

Jake grinned at them. He had made it. And what's more, he had helped save the *Flounder* and, with her, his friends.

The bilge

Captain Dreadnought strode up and down the deck, glaring at the crew who were lined up, grim-faced and silent. "This time we were lucky," said the Captain. "But we were caught on the hop. That storm should have been spied from forty knots. We could have sailed for shelter or furled the sails in before it got to us." He stopped. "Someone was off their watch. And that someone will be punished." He scanned the crew. "You might as well admit it or I'll get Saggers to check the log and then it'll be double punishment."

"It was me, sir," said Bill. Jake looked at him in horror.

The Captain took a step back. "Bill Baxter?

73

Are you sure?"

"Yes, sir. It was me. I lost track of time," insisted Bill.

"Very well," said Captain Dreadnought gravely. "Then you shall be punished accordingly. Saggers – take him to my cabin at once." Saggers went to grab Bill.

Jake had an awful sick feeling in his tummy, as if he had swallowed a very snotty oyster. This isn't right, he thought. It wasn't Bill's fault at all. He couldn't let him take the blame. And besides, surely the Captain would be lenient with Jake. He had saved the *Flounder*, after all. "It wasn't him," he said quietly. "It was me. It's my fault."

"What was that?" said Captain Dreadnought, peering down at Jake. "Did you say something?"

"Aye, sir," said Jake. "I missed my watch. It's my fault. I should be punished, not Bill."

The crew murmured and Jake heard someone say, "No!"

"That's enough!" snapped the Captain. "Be quiet or you'll all be punished." Then he turned back to Jake. "Well, well, well," he sneered.

"Jake Jellicoe. You've read the articles. Every single word, if I remember?"

Jake nodded.

"Then you'll know that deserting your duty is a serious offence and that I can do what I want with you."

Again Jake nodded.

"Hmm, let me see…" pondered Captain Dreadnought, twirling his moustache and drawing out the anticipation. "There's the gangplank, or 39 lashes, or maybe we could maroon him with some of Mrs Grimes's porridge."

"The bilge needs pumping," suggested Saggers, still stony-faced.

The Captain thought for a minute. "Yes, well, it will save someone else doing it, I suppose. We need the other hands to mend the rigging and patch the wood. Very well, Jake. You will be locked in the bilge until tomorrow morning, when I expect you to have pumped it clean. And as for the rest of you, no gawping! There's work to be done! I want to be digging up that treasure by the end of the week!" And he stamped off to his cabin.

"Come along, boy," said Saggers grimly. "It's the bilge for you."

The door slammed shut and Jake heard a bolt sliding home. He was standing in the bottom of the ship's hull, up to his knees in cold, brown seawater. He could feel things floating against him. Jake didn't know if they were dead or alive. He shivered.

"I'd better start pumping," he sighed. Taking a deep breath to fortify himself, he plunged his hands under the surface of the water to feel for the pump handle. "Aargh!" he cried as what he thought was the handle slithered away from him in an eel-like fashion. Carefully, he tried again and this time thankfully got hold of the real thing.

Jake began to pump. As he worked the handle up and down, pushing seawater back out to sea, he realized how sore his hands were. When he'd slid down the mast, he had been so numb with cold and fear that he hadn't felt the rope cut into his palms or the salt water sting the wounds. One of his nails had been ripped off completely. Salty tears began to run down Jake's cheeks and mix with the brine below. He thought of his family at home in Pollock Spit. Of Grandpa Jellicoe and his lost fortune. Of Ned and Fred who would still be complaining about their bellies. Of poor little Lily, two sizes too small. But mostly he thought about his ma. He had never wanted a hug so much in his life. It had been so long, maybe she had forgotten him. Jake tried to cheer himself up by thinking of the treasure. His want for it was huge. It sat like a knot in his tummy where hunger usually lurked. There would be sapphires and emeralds, diamond watches on golden chains, and coins, hundreds of coins. Jake thought so much about the treasure that before he knew it he had pumped the bilge dry. He sat down on an old bucket, leant against the pump handle and soon fell fast asleep.

Jake woke an hour later to a strange echoey sound creeping into the bilge. He sat up and listened harder. There it was again! It was coming from a wide pipe in the wall – one of the water chutes that let seawater out of the cabins upstairs and funnelled it down to the bilge below.

Jake got up and put his ear to the end of the pipe. He could hear someone talking. Someone unmistakably pompous and self-satisfied. It was Captain Dreadnought! The pipe must lead to his cabin. He seemed to be talking to someone, but Jake couldn't hear well enough to make out any replies. He put his whole head inside the pipe to hear better.

"Well, Hawkins, not long now," said Captain Dreadnought in a strangely sinister manner. "That treasure is just days away and then it will be like old times. Just you and me and our booty."

Who was Hawkins? Jake frowned. He carried on listening.

"At last I'll get my hands on my long-lost treasure. Think of it – a thousand sovereigns, jewels and gewgaws, all to ourselves. And if the crew thinks they're getting a brass razoo out of me then they're stupider than I thought. Don't they know they're dealing with the most feared pirate ever to plague the seven seas? We'll sail back to

Stinking Porth and I'll do for the lot of them before we reach shore. That way the world will know I'm back – and this time I mean business!" And he laughed a hideous laugh.

Jake pulled his head out of the pipe and sat down heavily on the bilge floor. He couldn't believe his ears. Captain Dreadnought wasn't from His Majesty's Navy at all. In fact, he wasn't even Captain Dreadnought! He was none other than the Dread Pirate Redbeard and he was planning to steal the crew's fortune and kill them all to boot! But how could this be true? After all, Redbeard was dead, wasn't he? And who exactly was this Hawkins who was in on the whole secret? Jake needed some answers and he needed them fast. He had to speak to Bill.

Hawkins

The lock clanked and slid and the bilge door opened. It was Saggers. "I assume you've learnt your lesson, boy?" he said.

Jake jumped to his feet. "Yes, sir," he said.

"Well, get moving then. There's work to be done on deck."

Jake hurried out of the bilge. He found Bill at the front of the ship painting the bowsprit, which had taken a battering in the storm.

Bill smiled as he saw Jake approaching. "All right, boy. You survived the bilge, then?"

Jake nodded.

"Well, you've lived through the worst storm for a hundred years – there's not much that can do for you now."

Jake gulped. Yesterday he would have agreed that he could beat anything. But now he knew they were all in mortal danger.

"You saw Redbeard," he said to Bill. "Tell me again what he looked like."

"Not again, Jake." Bill shook his head. "I've told you everything I know. It's these stories that got us all in trouble in the first place."

"But, Bill!" pleaded Jake.

"I told you. He was big. He had red hair and a red beard. Obviously. And he's as dead as a dodo now, so there's nothing for you to worry about."

"You must remember more."

"I was young, Jake, and scared. That's what I saw. Nothing more."

"Nothing?"

"No."

Jake hung his head. Bill was angry at him now. He started to walk away.

Bill watched him. "Wait," he said.

Jake turned back.

"There was something else. He had a bird on his shoulder. A big, black bird. A raven. Or a rook, maybe."

Jake gulped. "What was its name?" he said.

"Now, that I do remember," said Bill. "Hawkins. Its name was Hawkins."

The Captain's cabin

Jake felt sick with fear. He had to warn the crew that their lives were in danger. But Captain Dreadnought was sneaky and Jake knew he needed better evidence than overheard mutterings in the bilge pipe. He would have to break into the Captain's cabin.

Jake waited until the late watch, when the crew would be safely asleep dreaming of rum and their own mums, far away on dry land. The only man on watch was Pip Lloyd, and the sea was so calm that Jake knew he too would be snoring out on deck. So Jake hopped out of his bunk, crept up the steps and, as carefully as he could, opened the narrow door. He slid out before the moonlight disturbed any of the men below and clicked the door back into place.

Jake hurried along the deck and jumped down a hatch at the stern of the ship. He was heading for the bilge. The Captain slept in a special master bedroom at the front of the ship, and always locked his cabin at night, so the only way in would be the same way the noise had seeped out. He would have to climb up the bilge pipe. Jake ran through the galley, past the kitchen where Mrs Grimes sat slumped against the cold store, where she preferred to make her bed, with Ahab stretched out on her lap. Fast asleep, thought Jake. But he tiptoed past just in case.

But as he got to the door at the other end of the galley, the cook's lazy eye opened and she smiled nastily to herself.

Jake reached the bilge in the bottom of the boat. The pipe was wide – wide enough for someone as skinny as him, anyway. He stuck his head inside. Then, by pressing his hands and feet to the sides of the pipe, he managed to move up slowly, like a badly co-ordinated frog, until finally his head hit something hard. "Ow!" he said loudly. Then he said it again quietly and cursed himself for making such a noise. He'd cracked his head on the iron grille in the cabin floor. He'd made it! He pulled himself out and stood up. The Captain's oil lamp had been snuffed out, but enough moonlight streamed through the porthole to allow Jake to see.

On the desk sat Hawkins. Jake glared at him. The bird's beady glass eyes stared back. Jake crossed the room, but still the nasty raven seemed to be watching him.

"Stop it," said Jake. And he pulled a frilled shirt from the back of the door and hung it over the dome. "That's better," he said with a nod. "Now to work."

Jake began searching the Captain's cabin. On the desk he found a telescope for looking out to sea in an important manner. There was also a small comb – presumably for keeping the Captain's moustache neat, or maybe for brushing Hawkins's feathers? In the top drawer, Jake found a faded photograph of a lady in a revealing dress. "Pistol Patsy", it said underneath in Captain Dreadnought's elegant hand. Well, that was something. After all, how many navy captains knew girls called Pistol Patsy?

"Clue number one," murmured Jake.

In the second drawer, he found a gentleman's handkerchief with the initials D.P.R. monogrammed in the corner in gold thread.

Dread Pirate Redbeard! thought Jake. His second clue!

Then he looked around for more.

On the wall of the cabin hung a medicine cabinet with a mirror in the door. Jake opened it. Inside there were several bottles of Dr Rotter's Patented Ship's Medicine – guaranteed to cure seasickness, scurvy and salt-log. Jake wondered what salt-log was and if he had it. It sounded rather unpleasant. Then, just as he was imagining what awful things the disease was going to do to him, Jake noticed something else on the bottom shelf. He blinked and looked again to make sure. Then he smiled a wide smile. For there, in a neat row, were several bottles of hair dye. The label said: "Beetle Black. Covers all grey, brown and blond shades." Jake read the small print. "Tough on even the most unsightly of ginger hair-dos." Next to the boxes sat the Captain's razor. Jake picked it up carefully. Sure  enough, the edge of the blade was covered in tiny red shavings.

"He's been in disguise the whole time," said Jake to himself. "No wonder Bill didn't recognize him. Clue number three."

Jake looked further. On the velvet armchair he noticed a large leather-bound book with the words "Captain's Log" embossed on the cover. Jake sat down and opened it. The first few pages seemed harmless enough. "Wind: forty knots. Bound for the Equator," it said in Captain Dreadnought's neat hand.

Jake flicked through the pages, skimming the inky text. Then something caught his eye. On one page was a list headed "My pile". "Off Caracas" read the first entry. "Looted a schooner bound for the Spanish Main. Forty doubloons, three crew and a goat." The next entry was similar; only the location and amount of booty were different. This wasn't a log of the *Flounder* at all. This was a list of Redbeard's treasure. And it went on and on. There were all the boats he had plundered and the sailors he had sent to Davy Jones' locker. There were all the towns he had pillaged and left to rack and ruin.

Then Jake saw it. "Stinking Porth," it read. "A hundred pieces of eight, four gold rings and a talking turbot."

Jake felt sick. Grandpa's words echoed in his ears: "Wild red hair and a raven as black as coal". So it was Redbeard all along! He'd stolen Grandpa Jellicoe's fortune. Jake felt anger bubble up in his stomach. How could he? Grandpa had done nothing to him. He was a good man, kind and generous. Jake ripped the page out and stuffed it in his pocket.

"I'll get him," Jake said, aloud now. "I'll slice his fingers off and stick them on my own cap. I'll make him walk the gangplank with stones in his pockets so he sinks super-fast. I'll cover him in bananas and maroon him on that island of nasty winged monkeys!"

"Oh, you will, will you?" said a voice.

Jake swung round. The cabin door was open and there, lit by an oil lantern, was a terrifying silhouette. It was Redbeard – and behind him stood Saggers and Mrs Grimes.

"There he is," said Mrs Grimes. "I told you he was up to no good, creeping around like a rotten thief."

"Thank you, Mrs Grimes," said Captain Dreadnought. "You can go now. You too,

Saggers. Rouse the crew."

Jake watched in horror as Saggers and Mrs Grimes left the cabin, slamming the door shut behind them.

"I know all about you," Jake blurted out. "I've seen your hair dye and your razor with the red shavings."

Redbeard shot a look at the open medicine cabinet. He grabbed the razor, before lunging at Jake and holding the blade to his throat. Jake didn't dare breathe for fear of the metal cutting him.

"I could kill you right now if I wanted, boy," hissed Redbeard. "Slice you open from your gizzard to your navel. But then the rest of your idiot friends might get suspicious." And he pushed Jake away.

Jake felt his throat to make sure it was still intact. "You're a p...p... pirate," he stammered.

"I prefer to be known as a Gentleman of Fortune." Redbeard smiled. "So much more sophisticated, don't you think?"

"You stole my grandpa's money and his talking turbot," said Jake furiously.

Redbeard snorted. "So that fellow was your grandpa, was he? Well, well, well. Just like him, you are. Small and weedy with all the guts of a filleted herring."

"I'll tell them about you – Bill and Pip and the others," threatened Jake.

"You think they'll believe a little squirt like you? Anyway, they won't be able to hear you forty fathoms down."

"What do you mean?" asked Jake, trying to control the quiver in his voice.

"What I mean, dear boy," Redbeard said as he smiled a terrible smile, "is that you are going for a long walk … off a very short plank."

Walking the plank

Redbeard seized the monogrammed handkerchief out of Jake's hand and gagged him with it. Then, with a pair of stockings, he bound the boy's hands behind his back.

"That should keep you out of any more mischief till you're swimming with the fishes," sneered the Captain. Then he took Jake by the  scruff of the neck and marched him along the galley, up through the hatch and out onto the deck of the *Flounder*.

Pip Lloyd had woken up and was standing with Bill, Calico Jack,

Tom, Samuel, Charley, Richard and Christie. Behind them, on the poop deck, were Saggers and Mrs Grimes.

"Jake, what have you done?" said Bill.

Redbeard flung Jake towards him. "I found him pilfering in my own cabin. Trying to steal from me, he was. Trying to get his fingers on the map so he could keep the treasure all himself."

The crew gasped.

"No, Jake," said Bill.

"Yes," said Redbeard.

"He's lying!" cried Jake. "He's the real villain. He's not who you think he is. He's not Captain Dreadnought at all…"

But all the crew heard was, "Hhhmph gggle mmmmm."

"What was you doing, boy?" said Pip.

"How did he get into the cabin?" demanded Bill, suspicious.

"Up the bilge pipe," replied Redbeard. "The little rat must have been sneaking around in there the other night when he was supposed to be pumping."

"Is that true, Jake?" asked Bill.

Jake nodded sadly.

"Oh, Jake," said Bill, shaking his head.

"Yes, well, enough of this chitchat," said Redbeard. "This is where we go our separate ways. We're going to find the treasure. And you're going to the bottom of the briny."

"Nnnnggggg!" said Jake.

"No!" said Bill.

"Yes," said Redbeard. "He's going down the gangplank."

"That ain't fair. He's just a boy," protested Bill.

"He knows the rules like the rest of you," snapped Redbeard. "You'd better keep it buttoned from now on, Bill Baxter, or you'll be joining him. Now, Jellicoe, are you going to walk or do I have to get Saggers to push you?"

Jake sniffed and shook his head. If he was going to go, it would be with pride. He stepped onto the long piece of oak he'd walked up all those months ago.

"Goodbye, Jake," said Bill solemnly. "We'll never forget you."

"Goodbye, boy," said the crew, their faces fallen and their eyes filled with horror.

As Jake walked slowly along the plank, one step at a time, Pip Lloyd began to sing a sad song of lost love in a land far away. Jake blinked away the tears that were seeping out. At last, he reached the end. He looked down to the swirling sea below. If the fall didn't kill him, then the giant squid or man-eating whales surely would.

Jake shut his eyes.

"Sorry, Grandpa," he said. "Sorry, Ma." Then he took one last step forward and walked into nothing. Time seemed to stand still for a minute before he felt himself plunging into the dark, icy fathoms, black as coal soup and colder than

death. Jake felt his fingers and toes freezing …
then his whole body went numb… Then he felt
nothing at all.

Boris Kalashnikov

"**W**ake up, boy," said the voice.

Jake ignored it. He was dead, wasn't he? He could do what he liked if he was dead.

"Oy. I said wake up." Then whatever was attached to the voice kicked him in the shin.

Jake opened his eyes. Above him bright blue spread out to fill the sky. Then a gigantic face came into view. It had an eye patch and the biggest, bushiest hairdo Jake had ever seen. Then he realized it wasn't a hairdo at all. The face was upside down. The hairdo was a beard. Jake sat up, coughing and spluttering. A small fish shot out of his mouth.

"So 'e is alive," said the giant.

"B... B... B..."

"What is it, boy?"

"B… B… Boris Kalashnikov!" stammered Jake. "Aaaarghh!" he cried and scrabbled backwards to escape.

Boris laughed. "Well, that's the thanks I get for saving his life, is it?" He turned to a gang of sailors behind him, all of whom wore eye patches and had hooks where their left hands should have been.

"But… But…" stammered Jake again. "You'll grate my feet and make me eat the shavings."

Boris and his crew laughed again. "What else have they told you?" asked the giant pirate.

"That you'll let rats nibble my ears and worms

wriggle up my nostrils and that you once ate someone's grandma."

"Oh, I am disappointed." Boris shook his head. "Shall we tell him, boys?" he said to the crew.

"Go on, Captain!" said one of the pirates. "If ye trust him."

Boris turned to Jake. "Swear loyalty to me, boy. If not, I'll send you back to Davy Jones' Locker, where you was headed."

Jake had no choice. He could either die now, or die later. He chose later. "I swear," he said.

"I am a pirate," said Boris. "That much is true. But the rest of the tales you've been told are naught but myth and legend. My real name is Percy Arkwright."

"So why do you call yourself Boris Kalashnikov?" asked Jake, puzzled.

"Well, who'd be afeared of the Dread Pirate Arkwright?" said Boris, shaking his head.

Jake had to admit he had a point. "Are you really a pirate?" he asked.

"In a way," said Boris. "But I only steal from the rich and nasty, and give most of it to the poor. The rest we share equally among ourselves –

call it commission, if you like."

"Like Robin Hood," said Jake.

"I like to think so," said Boris.

"What about the eye patches?" asked Jake.

"Just for show," said Boris.

"And the hooks?"

"Fake. How do you think we'd rig a ship if all of us had pointy bits of iron in the way all the time?"

The crew took off their hooks to reveal their left hands.

"Gosh!" said Jake. "What about the grating?"

"Cheese only," said Boris. "But it makes for a gruesome story, doesn't it? Enough to keep every ship on the ocean out of my way and stop them trying to sink me."

Jake thought for a minute. This was great. But something was bothering him. "Why doesn't any-one tell?" he asked, looking at the pirate crew.

"Why would they?" said Boris. "They lead a good life aboard a good ship. They earn good money – more than they could earn on any other boat and more than if they were landlubbers."

Jake looked around him. It made sense now.

"I've told you my story," said Boris. "Fair's fair. You tell us yours."

So Jake told Boris everything. About the Jellicoes and the new baby that was going to be sold. About Grandpa and the talking turbot and how his fortune had been stolen. About Bill and the others and how they'd taught him to sail the *Flounder*. About what he'd overheard that night in the bilge. And about the photo and the hair dye and the red shavings on the razor and Captain Dreadnought's secret.

"I knew it," thundered Boris. "I knew he was still alive."

Lastly, Jake told him how he'd been caught and made to walk the plank.

"And that's when we saved you," said Boris.

"Well, you tried to kill him first," said one of the pirates.

Boris looked shamefaced. "I did, yes. But only because I thought you were a small whale. I harpooned you, see. But I caught your jacket instead and hooked you up and blow me if instead of a big fish you weren't a very small boy who looked like he'd been at sea for days."

"Are you sure he's telling the truth?" said another man. "He could be making it up. He could be a spy for Redbeard."

"I'm not," said Jake. "I'm not a spy. It's all true, every last word of it." Then he remembered. "The handkerchief!" he cried. "He gagged me with it. Where is it?"

"You mean this?" asked Boris, holding out a sodden grey square.

Jake grabbed it and looked for the monogram. "Here!" he cried. "D. P. R. – Dread Pirate Redbeard!"

"Hmm," said Boris. "Maybe. Or it could be Deirdre Penelope Rooster. Or Denzil Pewsey Ribblethwaite."

"But why would he have their hankies?" asked Jake, exasperated. Then he thought of something. "Wait," he said. "There's something else as well. He reached inside his trouser pocket and pulled out a very wet piece of paper, which he handed to Boris.

"Here," he said. "It's the log of all the ships he's looted."

Boris took the list and unfolded it. "So it is," he said. "So it is."

Jake stared at the piece of paper. "Hang on," he said. There was something on the back – a diagram Jake hadn't seen before. "Look – what's that?"

Boris turned the piece of paper over. He frowned with concentration. Then gradually the frown disappeared and an enormous grin spread across his hairy face. "Well, shiver me timbers, Jake. It's the map! The map of Redbeard's treasure! Look!"

Jake looked. On the paper was drawn an island with small pictures to indicate trees and a river. In the middle was a big black cross marked with the words "Here lyes treasure".

"Crikey," said Jake.

"This is the most precious piece of wet paper in history," said Boris. "Now, we find the treasure and get it back to its rightful owners. But it won't be easy," he warned. "Redbeard will have memorized every inch of this map. Plus, he's been there before, so our advantage is only tiny. We have to set sail immediately."

"Can I come too?" asked Jake.

"You, my boy, are the guest of honour. You can share the Captain's cabin with me."

Then Boris called out to his hook-handed crew. "Turn her about, boys! We're heading for the treasure island!"

Treasure Island

T he *Molotov* sailed for a week and a day
towards the island. The crew were as kind to
Jake as Bill and Pip and the others had been.
Kindest of all was Boris himself, who taught
Jake how to navigate through the black-painted
galley and passages, who let him have the top
hammock in his cabin and who always gave him
an extra helping of ship's biscuits at supper.

Jake's job on board was to man the crow's nest
– a small basket near the top of the foremast. A
few months ago, Jake would rather have eaten
Mrs Grimes's revolting meat surprise than spend
a whole day high up in the sky like that, but after
the storm he knew he could tackle anything. He
grew to love the bird's-eye view of the world, the

wind blowing through his hair and the gulls swooping and squawking around him. As he scanned the horizon, looking for the island and watching the sea slip away behind him, he saw magnificent humpback whales blowing spouts of water up into the air. He saw shoals of silvery haddock flit through the water as if they were birds flocking through the air. He saw poisonous jellyfish and deadly barracuda and at night he saw the sea light up with spooky phosphorescence. And finally he saw what he had been waiting for.

"Land ahoy!" he shouted.

There it was. A small spit of sand with trees in the centre and, rising behind them, a large rock. Somewhere, amongst it all, lay the treasure.

"Come down, boy!" shouted Boris.

Jake clambered down the mast as nimbly as a monkey and jumped onto the deck. "We're here!" he said. "We've made it. And there's no sign of the *Flounder*."

"Good work," said Boris and he hugged Jake. "The crew will anchor up the *Molotov*, and you and I will set for shore in the lifeboat to find the treasure."

"OK!" said Jake excitedly.

Boris and Jake climbed into the wooden rowing boat that had been hung above deck the whole voyage, waiting for this very day. The pirate crew pulled on a giant wooden lever and the boat swung out over the sea. Then, slowly and creakily, they were lowered onto the water.

"I'll row," said Boris "You take the tiller." And with Boris's giant arms pulling on the oars and

Jake's skinny ones steering them steadily, they whizzed across the water to the shore of the treasure island.

Soon they were wading through the shallows, pulling the boat behind them.

Boris hauled the vessel all the way up the beach. "So it doesn't wash away and maroon us here," he said wisely.

Jake nodded.

"Now, let's look at that map," said Boris, rubbing his hands together.

Jake fished in his jacket pocket, pulled out the piece of paper, unfolded it and smoothed it out onto a rock. It was a bit dog-eared and the ink had run in places. But the X was still clear.

"Which direction are we pointing in?" said Boris. "I'm terrible at navigation, you know. If you need fearsome growling and sheer brute strength then I'm your man, but if you're looking for north-north-west at a 30-degree latitude then I'm stumped. Maybe we should just start walking."

"No, wait," said Jake. "Here." And from his

trouser pocket he pulled out the compass he had brought from home.

"By jiminy, you're full of surprises, boy," laughed Boris.

Jake held out the tiny round globe in front of him and watched as the needle spun furiously on its axis before pointing in one direction. "That's north," said Jake. "And look, north is shown on the map, which means we must be at this bit of beach." He pointed to a wiggly line at the bottom of the picture. "So we have to walk straight ahead until we reach the trees and then diagonally to our right until we find the clearing."

Boris jumped to his feet. "Let's go," he said. "Here, hop up." And he leant forward so that Jake could sit on his shoulders. "It'll be quicker this way. You read the map and compass and shout down directions."

"OK!" said Jake.

"Off we go," said Boris and set off towards the forest, giant step by giant step.

Who would have known it? thought Jake as he rode on Boris's shoulders through the woods.

Who would think that somewhere so unimportant-looking was the richest piece of land on earth, hiding such a secret.

Boris plodded on.

"Stop!" Jake called as they came out into a clearing. "Now turn to your right one step."

Boris did as he was told.

"Forward two steps."

Boris walked forward two steps.

"Hmm. Back half a step," said Jake. "I think we went a bit too far."

Boris shuffled back slightly.

"This is it!" cried Jake. "X marks the spot. This is the spot, right in front of us."

Boris lowered Jake onto the ground and they looked at the sand. "Get the shovel, boy," said the pirate.

"Er, what shovel?" said Jake.

"Oh," said Boris. "Damn. I think, in all the excitement, I might have forgotten the tools." He put his head in his hands. "What a big lummox," he said.

But Jake smiled. "We don't need a shovel," he said. "Your hands are huge. Look."

Boris looked. It was true. His hands were the size of dinner plates. He laughed. "To work!" he cried and began to dig at the silvery sand, moving bucketfuls behind him with every scoop. Jake joined in, throwing small handfuls to the side.

For hours they dug, until they were both so deep in the sand Boris could only just see over the top.

"Maybe I misread the map," said Jake sadly. "Or maybe the map was for something else."

"No," insisted Boris. "Come on. It's here somewhere, I can smell it."

Jake scooped up another handful of sand and was just about to fling it over the top when something flashed in the sunlight. "Look!" he said.

Boris held Jake's hand in front of him and poked at the sand. Then he pulled out a shiny object and held it up to the light. It spangled, sending rays of sun beaming out around the pit. "Well, I'll be blowed," said Boris. "It's a ring. A diamond ring. We've found it. We've found the treasure!"

Jake dug again and pulled out a necklace of

clear green stones fastened with a silver clasp.

"Emeralds," said Boris. "Keep digging. They must have spilled out of the chest. That's what we're after. That's where the real treasure is hidden." He started shovelling again.

Jake couldn't think what could be more real than diamonds and emeralds, but he dug anyway until finally Boris stubbed his thumb on something very solid.

"Ow!" said the pirate.

"What is it?" asked Jake.

"I think I may have hit something," said Boris. And he scraped away the sand.

Jake's heart leapt. There in front of them was a large wooden box with brass bands stretched across the lid. In the centre was a plaque with a name engraved in swirly letters: PROPERTY OF D. P. REDBEARD.

"It's the chest!" cried Jake. "Redbeard's treasure chest!"

Boris reached around the vast trunk and hauled it up out of the sand. Then, using his bare hands, he snapped the lock open. Slowly and carefully, as if scared of what he might find, he lifted the lid.

The bright light that shone from the chest blinded Jake for a second, making him blink and turn away. Then, shielding his eyes, he looked again. "Wow," he gasped.

"Har-har me hearties!" cried Boris.

Inside the trunk was more gold and silver and precious stones than Jake thought existed in the whole world. There were earrings and cufflinks and toe rings. There were silver baubles and gold trinkets and enough jewellery to bedeck the neck and wrists of every princess from Xanadu to Zanzibar. But mostly there were coins. Hundreds and thousands of gold coins, lighting up the dark hole with their yellow glow.

Jake dipped his fingers into the chest. It was deep and cold and delicious.

"Feels good, doesn't it?" said a voice. But it didn't belong to Boris. It was another tone, less gruff, more flamboyant and very, very familiar. Jake looked up. At the top of the hole, hands on his hips, legs wide apart, stood Redbeard. "Boris Kalashnikov, we meet again," he said.

"Redbeard!" cried Jake. "But I was in the crow's nest and the *Flounder* was nowhere to be seen."

"That's because we came the back route. First pirate rule: never take the obvious course – you'll always get caught."

Boris shook his head. "Redbeard!" he thundered. "Why, I should—"

"What you should do," interrupted Redbeard, "is shut your big hairy mouth right now. I have a very large pistol in my hand and I can assure you that it is loaded. But that wouldn't be as much fun as what I have in mind – so I want you both out of that pit this instant. And bring my treasure with you."

Scowling angrily, Boris picked up Jake in one arm and the chest in the other and deposited both at the surface before heaving himself up as well.

"Jake," said another voice, kinder this time. "Is it really you?"

Jake looked round. "Bill?" he said.

"Yes, it's me! I can't believe you're alive!" Bill ran to Jake, picked him up and hugged him tight.

"Bill? Bill Baxter? Son of Josiah Baxter, former carpenter on the good ship *Molotov*?" It was Boris.

"Boris," replied Bill, setting Jake down gently. "It's good to see you again."

"Hang on," said Jake. "What's going on? I don't understand."

"Nor do I," said Redbeard, sounding annoyed.

"Jake, remember I told you that Redbeard had snatched my father from the ship I was sailing on?"

Jake nodded.

"Well, that ship was the *Molotov*. I was Boris's cabin boy. The day Redbeard kidnapped my dad, I vowed to hunt him down and make him pay for what happened. And I knew the only way to do that, to make sure that I really hurt him, was to steal his treasure. So, when he advertised for crew on the *Flounder*, I signed up."

"But how did you know it was him?" asked Jake.

"Yes, how?" asked Redbeard.

"I didn't at first," said Bill to the pirate. "I just signed up on any ship in the hope that one day I'd meet you. But after you made Jake walk the plank I got suspicious. As the weeks passed I began to see more clues. The way your temper flared up.

The pirate words that you used. Your pale skin, always wearing a hat to shade yourself."

"Damn yer eyes!" exclaimed Redbeard.

"You knew before, didn't you, Jake? That's why you were in his cabin." Bill looked at the boy.

Jake nodded.

"I'm sorry you had to walk the plank. I thought he was just following ship's rules," said Bill.

"That's OK," said Jake. "Boris saved me."

"All this reminiscing is very pleasant, but I'm going to take my treasure now," said Redbeard.

"It's not yours," said Boris. "It belongs to the hundreds of people you stole it from. And anyway, we were here first."

"That's right," said Jake and stood with Boris. Bill joined them.

"There are three of us and only one of you, so you're outnumbered," said Jake.

"Hmm," said Redbeard and pulled out his pistol. "But if I use this there'll be none of you. So I win."

"No," said Bill. "If we fight, we fight fair, like true seamen."

"That's right," said Boris. "We'll have a duel. Just you and me."

Redbeard smiled wickedly to himself. "Very well," he said. "A duel."

The duel

Redbeard and Boris stood back to back on the sand, their pistols at the ready.

"Now, men," said Bill. "Though I use the word 'man' loosely in your case, Redbeard, you heartless sea dog."

"Get on with it," snapped the pirate.

"Very well," said Bill. "You will each take ten paces forward. Then, on the tenth and final pace, you will turn and shoot. The deadlier shot will win the treasure. The loser will die a painful death."

Jake covered his eyes. This was awful. Why couldn't they have a nice game of chess or backgammon or another game that was less bloody and gruesome?

"Start your pacing!" shouted Bill.

Boris and Redbeard began to take large, bold steps.

"How many is that?" asked Boris after a few.

"Oh, for heaven's sake," said Redbeard. "If he can't count, I should win by default."

"Put a sock in it," said Bill.

"Er, so how many is it?" asked Boris again.

"Now I've lost count with all the talking," snapped Redbeard. "Start again."

So the two men stamped back to the middle.

"I'll count aloud," volunteered Jake.

"Good boy," said Bill.

So Jake began to count. "One," he said.

The two men took a step away from each other.

"Two," Jake continued. "Three."

He began to feel a bit sick. What if Boris lost? Then Redbeard would get the treasure

120

and Boris would be dead and Jake and Bill would be next.

"Four," he said a little shakily.

But if Boris won then all Jake's dreams would come true. The Dread Pirate Redbeard would be dead and Bill would have avenged his father, Boris would have money for the poor and Jake would have his fortune to buy back the baby.

"Five," he said more boldly. "Six."

The pirates put their hands onto their pistols, ready to draw.

"Seven," said Jake. "Eight." He took a deep breath, but as he did so, he saw something awful. Redbeard began to turn. He wasn't waiting for Jake to count to ten. He was going to shoot Boris in the back in cold blood.

Redbeard put his finger on the trigger and slowly pulled —

"Noooooo!" shouted Jake.

Boris swung round. A shot fired. And as it did so Jake, without thinking, leapt into the air between Boris and Redbeard – into the path of the bullet.

"Jake!" yelled Bill.

But it was too late. The bullet sped through the air and hit Jake's chest. The boy fell to the floor with an awful thud.

There was silence. Then Boris pulled out his pistol and started towards Redbeard. "You cheating devil!" he thundered. "You've killed an innocent boy for your greed. And now I'm going to kill you!"

"Innocent?" laughed Redbeard. "That boy was a common thief and a sneak."

Boris snatched Redbeard's pistol from his hand, hoisted him up by the neck of his shirt and held the gun to his head. "This is for all the women and children who you've robbed of money and jewels and precious husbands, sons and brothers," he said.

"And for Grandpa Jellicoe," added a small voice.

"And for him as well," said Boris. Then he realized what he'd heard. "Jake!" he said, looking down at the boy.

"Jake?" said Bill. "Holy Moses, he's alive!"

And he was. Jake sat up and dusted the sand off himself.

"How on earth did you manage that?" asked Boris.

"Oh, he's survived the worst storm for a century," said Bill. "He's an amazing boy."

"He certainly is," sneered Redbeard.

Boris released his grip on Redbeard's shirt and dropped him to the ground.

"Owww," said Redbeard as his bottom hit the sand.

"That's nothing," snarled Boris. "If you try anything again, I'll grate your eyelids and feed 'em to the fishes. Now, keep still while I tie you up good and proper." And he lashed Redbeard's hands together with a piece of string he always kept for such purposes.

"But how?" asked Bill as he knelt beside Jake.

"Well, the bullet did hit me," said Jake. "But something got in the way." He reached into his jacket pocket and pulled out something hard and round and flat. Grandpa's coin! It had saved his life and had a large bullet-sized dent to prove it.

"Well, you know what this means, don't you?" said Boris.

"We have to start again?" said Jake.

"No," said Boris. "We've won. Redbeard cheated, so he forfeits the treasure. You've done it, Jake. You've found your fortune."

Jake turned to Bill. "Is that true?" he said.

Bill nodded.

"Hang on, don't I have a say?" spluttered Redbeard.

"No," said Bill. "Not any more. In fact no one will hear anything you have to say ever again."

"Why not?" asked Redbeard.

"You are going to enjoy a very long holiday in a nice hot climate with your own private beach," said Bill with a smile.

"You mean..."

"That's right," continued Boris. "We're marooning you. You can stay here until the gulls peck out your eyes and eat your liver for breakfast."

"No!" cried Redbeard. "It gets so lonely and dark and there are strange noises at night."

"Goodbye," said Boris and he hoisted the gigantic chest up onto his shoulder.

"No, wait! Come back, come back!" shouted Redbeard.

But it was too late. Bill and Jake and Boris had gone.

Goodbye, Boris

At the beach Boris put down the chest and opened the lid. He scooped up a handful of coins and jewels and held them out to Jake. "This is your grandpa's share," he said. "Redbeard stole it and it's rightfully yours."

Jake held out his hands and let the treasure flood in. "Thank you!" he said as he stuffed it in his pockets and in his shoes.

Boris scooped up another handful. "Bill, this is for you – to make up for the loss of your father Josiah."

But Bill shook his head. "No thanks," he said. "I don't need money. I did what I came to do – and that was to see Redbeard suffer. There are others need it more than me."

"Very noble of you," said Boris. "But your crew will want paying. They're honest men and they were promised a share of the booty, so here it is. I've enough here for Redbeard's other victims – the ones who are still alive anyway – and for my men too. Here." And he poured another scoop into Bill's hands.

Bill smiled. "Imagine their faces!" he said.

"Now you'd better get your lifeboat ready," said Boris. "I need to say goodbye to Jake."

Bill nodded and left the two of them alone.

Boris crouched down so that he was closer to Jake. "This is where we go our separate ways," he said. "But I've got something else to tell you – a secret that not even Bill knows."

Jake looked at Boris quizzically.

"I've found my next Boris," he said.

Jake was confused. "What do you mean?"

"I'm not the first Boris Kalashnikov," said the pirate. "Nor will I be the last. The seas will always need someone like me to look out for the little people. Them that can't fight back against villains like Redbeard. When I'm old and grey and ready to retire to a nice bungalow in Florida, and when you're a man, I'll sail to Pollock Spit and find you. Then you, Jake Jellicoe, can be the next Dread Pirate Kalashnikov. You can steal from the rich and give to the poor. Just like Robin Hood."

"I will," said Jake, his heart bursting with excitement. "I will."

"Until then, you look after your ma. And your new little sister or brother."

Jake gasped. "The baby! I'd better get going." He flung his arms around Boris and gave him a hug.

"Go on," said Boris. "But let this be a warning. If you ever tell my secret, then I will know, and I will find you, wherever you are, and it will be more than cheese I am grating."

Jake gulped and shook his head. "I'll never tell. I swear."

"Good boy," said Boris. "Quick now, Bill's waiting."

"Goodbye," said Jake.

"Goodbye," said Boris.

So Jake joined Bill in the lifeboat and rowed towards the *Flounder*, while Boris set off for the

Molotov. But when Jake turned to wave across the water, Boris was already gone.

A new captain

The crew of the *Flounder* were delighted to see Jake again and even happier when Bill told them the truth about Captain Dreadnought and how he had plotted to kill them all and keep the treasure for himself.

"So where is it, then?" asked Pip Lloyd.

"Aye," said Tom. "Where's the loot?"

"Here it is, boys," said Bill and he emptied his pockets, showering the deck with gold coins, rings and bangles.

The sailors whooped with delight and ran back and forth grabbing at the treasure.

"There's plenty to go round, so no fighting," added Bill. "Even enough for you, Saggers."

The First Mate stood poker-faced watching

130

the proceedings. "I don't deserve anything," he said.

"No, he doesn't," agreed Jake. "He helped Redbeard!"

"But he didn't know it was the Dread Pirate. He thought he was being loyal to his captain," said Bill. "Didn't you?"

Saggers nodded.

"He did a good job, really, when you think about it," said Bill.

Jake thought about it. He wasn't so sure. But Bill knew best.

"This leaves us with one problem," said Bill.

"What?" asked Jake, wondering what on earth could be the matter now.

"We need a new captain," said Bill.

"Well, that's easy," said Pip. "You should do it, Bill."

"No, not me," said Bill. "I'm a carpenter, nothing more, nothing less. It should be Jake."

"Me?" asked Jake.

"Him?" asked the crew incredulously.

"Yes," said Bill. "He survived the storm, halfway up the foremast. He survived walking the plank. He even survived Redbeard's bullet and the dreaded Boris Kalashnikov." He gave Jake a quick wink. "And he brought you back the treasure. I can think of no one finer to steer the *Flounder* back to Stinking Porth."

So that is exactly what Jake did. With Pip as the new Quartermaster and Mrs Grimes relegated to cleaning duty, he captained the *Flounder* back across the seven seas to home. They sailed steadily with a trade wind behind them until, a few weeks later, the cry went up from Charley Farley in the crow's nest. "Land ahoy!"

The prodigal son

Jake walked up the narrow, cobbled street, his sea legs feeling very wobbly on solid land after six months away.

He reached the familiar tall, thin house, and knocked on the door.

"Coming," said an old man's voice from inside. "I'm old and slow and my knees are gammy, so you'll have to be patient."

Grandpa Jellicoe poked his head round the door. "What do you want, boy?" he said to Jake. "I've no money for hotcakes or whatever it is you're selling."

"Grandpa, it's me," said Jake.

"Jake?" said Grandpa, peering closer. "By gumbo, it is you!" And he grabbed Jake's hands and danced him in a circle. "Look at you, boy. I hardly recognized you. You're as brown as a nut and your hair is so blond. And you're six inches taller!"

"I've been at sea," said Jake.

Grandpa sighed happily. "Oh, it's good to see you. We've missed you around here."

Jake fished in his pocket and pulled out the gold coin with the bullet dent in it. "Here," he said. "You can have it back. It saved my life."

"Thanks, Jake," said Grandpa. "We could certainly use it round here." Jake saw tears in his eyes as the old man rubbed the coin between his fingers.

"You don't under-stand, Grandpa," said Jake. "Look." And he turned out his pockets. Gold and rubies and sapphires as big as eggs tumbled to the ground. "It's your fortune, Grandpa," said Jake. "I got it back for you.

From Redbeard. It was him, wasn't it?"

Grandpa stared wide-eyed at the booty. "Redbeard. That was his name, was it? Well, it suited him," he whispered. "No one believed me," he added. "But it was true."

"I believed you," said Jake. "Is it enough, do you think?"

"Enough? What do you want to buy – a palace?" said Grandpa.

"No, I just want to get my little brother or sister back," replied Jake.

"Lawks! Your ma!" cried Grandpa. "She's in hospital right now. Hurry, before she hands the little mite over."

Jake and Grandpa Jellicoe collected the booty and put it in Jake's treasure box for safe keeping. Then they ran as fast as their legs could carry them down the hill to the hospital.

The Jellicoes' fortune

And that's how Jake thwarted the Dread Pirate Redbeard and won back Grandpa's fortune.

The Jellicoes sold the tall, thin house and bought a bigger one, where everyone had a proper bouncy bed with a feather eiderdown and pillows and no one had to sleep in a drawer or the pantry or the coal scuttle. Best of all, Jake got to share his room with his new baby brother, Billy, named after the best ship's carpenter ever to set sail from Stinking Porth. They bought an automatic floor-washing machine for the fish market, so Mr Jellicoe could stay at home and look after the baby,

while Mrs Jellicoe made jam, which she sold in jars labelled JELLICOE JAM. And it truly was the best thing Jake had ever tasted. Gloopy sweet stuff, thick with red fruit and sugar.

Jake worked hard at school and even harder down at the docks at weekends, where Bill taught him all he knew about sailing ships and the sea.

Neither of them ever told anyone the truth about Boris. But every evening Jake would gaze out of his bedroom window, out to sea, looking for the black sails of the *Molotov* sailing in to Pollock Spit.

And what about Redbeard? Some say his eyes were pecked out by gulls and that he wandered blind around the island until he dried up into no more than bones. Others say he was picked up by a passing merchant ship that later sank off Cape Horn in a terrible gale. But everyone was sure of one thing. He was in Davy Jones' locker, which was the best place for such a terrible man.

Epilogue

A few years later, in a corner shop near the docks of a big city in America, a small oblong card appeared. On it, in neat, swirly lettering, was the following advert:

WANTED
Cabin Boy
Aboard the good ship Amelia
Must be small and strong with good sea legs.
Apply Capt. Dreadnought.

In the Kingdom of Elsewhere, just to the left of Nomansland and not far from Xanadu, sits Royal Nerdal Norton – a town so small and insignificant that only the gods and mapmakers have heard of it. And now you, of course.

The town of Royal Nerdal Norton has a problem. Small brown monkeys are causing all manner of mischief and bother, and not even Maurice Hankey, the incompetent court magician, or Terry Bunce, the haphazard inventor, can help. So it's up to Solomon Smee, a small boy with brown-rimmed glasses and dark, dark hair, to save the day!